The Valley
of Whispers

Karla Brading

Pont

For Willow

First published in 2016 by Pont Books, an imprint of
Gomer Press, Llandysul, Ceredigion, SA44 4JL
www.gomer.co.uk

ISBN 978 1 78562 170 3

A CIP record for this title is available from the British Library.

This book is published with the financial support
of the Welsh Books Council.

Printed and bound in Wales at Gomer Press,
Llandysul, Ceredigion.

Chapter One

STARING AT the grey fog from the cool wooden floor of the assembly hall, he mouthed the words to a hymn – something about creatures great and small. He wasn't keen on singing. Singing was for girls in pretty dresses, skipping ropes and braided hair. So he pretended he was absorbed in the music as he watched a blackbird balancing on a wire outside the window, eyeing the ground for crumbs.

When the old piano keys stopped tinkling, he snapped his attention back to the front of the hall. Assembly was over. The younger *kids were being ushered out and classes were about to begin. Maths first. Pah! He hated sums. Especially subtractions. There was something about that minus sign he didn't like. He'd seen it on his mam's letters at home – when she looked at them spread across the kitchen table, hands turning in her lap and skin ghost white.*

'I think it's going to rain,' he could hear a classmate mumble behind him.

'It always rains in Wales,' he'd heard his mam say on the phone once. He was starting to think she wasn't wrong.

✳

Tomas opened one bleary eye. There wasn't any fog outside like in his dream. The summer was still there to lure him outside and the world was full of colour: trees full of pink blossoms; blue cloudless skies with white, puffy airplane trails; tufts of greeny-yellowy

6

grass that had been mowed and left in piles around the fields.

He lifted his head from his pillow and felt the fuzzy murk of sleep in his brain struggling to vanish as his thoughts of getting ready took over.

Last day, he told himself. Just one more day and I'll be free.

The teachers had told them they could wear whatever they wanted. No boring green polo shirt and black trousers. He opted for his Spiderman T-shirt – designed to look like he was actually the superhero himself – and a pair of jeans, already neatly ironed by his mam in his little chest of drawers. At his old school in Cardiff, they'd never had 'no school uniform days'. It was always smart trousers and shirts; blazers when it got cold with shirt buttons done right up to your chin. There'd been no room for movement *whatsoever*, and Tomas had hated it.

At the breakfast table, he found his mam

with a mug of coffee. She was staring at the kettle as if it was going to mutate into something nasty and bite her head off.

'Mam?' Tomas called. 'Maaaam?!'

When she ignored him, he sometimes resorted to calling her by her first name. *Then* she usually listened . . .

'Carys!'

She turned to him sharply. '*What*?'

'It's no school uniform day, okay?'

'I know,' she replied, with a sleepy yawn. 'I had a letter about it.'

'Just checking,' Tomas said, reaching for a bowl from the lower cupboard.

Making breakfast was always one of his proudest moments, now that he was allowed to fix his cornflakes without supervision. He had sat patiently at the table every morning for so many years, pressing his fingernails into the gone-off fruit and watching the juices bubbling beneath the skin. Mam had been pretty angry when she'd reached for a pear one day and spotted the half-moon piercings in the fruit's flesh. She'd stopped his desserts for three whole days for wasting – even though the fruit had looked brown and soggy in the first place!

Shaking off the memory, Tomas' cereal *clink-clink-clinked* into the bottom of the bowl and in his haste, he splashed milk all over the countertop. His mam didn't notice the mess. She was staring out the window, where a fresh batch of clean washing had been pegged on the line the night before. The clothing fluttered in the wind, waving like flags in celebration for the approaching school holidays. She'd been lucky it hadn't rained in the night.

Tomas mopped the milk up with a tea towel and dumped it back on the side.

When his cornflakes – an inch thick in sugar due to eager spoonfuls from the canister – had all been crunched up and his rucksack packed with crisps, chocolate bars and boring ham sandwiches, his mam grabbed her handbag and waved him to the door.

'Mam, the key!' Tomas pointed out. She'd almost slammed the door shut with the key still in the lock on the inside. It wouldn't be the first time she'd done it.

'Shoot!' she hissed. 'That's me rushing, see,' she complained to herself.

'I can walk on my own if you want?' Tomas suggested. 'I won't be alone. I'd knock for James.'

'No. I like the exercise,' she replied, picking up the pace as if to prove it.

His mam was a slim woman – tall and pretty, though a little tired looking. She had heavy bags under her eyes that she covered thickly in make-up and she used brown-coloured lipsticks instead of the bright reds on adverts. Her hair was long and thick, brown-blonde in colour with a hint of grey poking through at the top of her centre parting. When she smiled, she had dimples in her cheeks. Tomas always liked to see them there; a true mark of her happiness. But lately, they'd been hiding.

At school, he was quick to wave goodbye to her. He joined his new friends in the playground – slipping in a quick and boisterous game of footy – whilst lingering parents gossiped on the outskirts. He could see his mam amongst them. Her friend, Samantha, was there with her little girl in a pram. Often they'd walk back together and round off the morning with a coffee at Megabytes Café.

'Like the T-shirt,' one of the boys said, touching the material with a grin as Tomas closely observed the ball bouncing between his team-mates. 'Have you seen the new film yet?'

'Nah, not yet,' he replied, before darting off for a sneaky tackle that won him the ball. He passed it on quickly and studied its progress like an astrologist intently watching stars.

Tomas wasn't hugely into football. Not like most of the boys in his village. He didn't follow a team or collect the stickers. He'd just found it was the quickest and easiest route to making friends, when he'd timidly arrived a few months back. Games made him feel good, especially when the lads called his name to join in. It was better than standing around doing nothing and he embraced the chance to burn off energy with people who wanted to share it with him.

'Hey Tom!' came a cry in the distance. James was flailing his arms about in greeting, dressed in a camouflage T-shirt and a pair of jogging bottoms that were loosely tied at the front. His trainers were covered in blades of cut grass and buttercup petals. He didn't like to stick to the concrete path. He was an adventurer, Tomas had discovered. If James could avoid being normal, he did.

Tomas waved back, missing the ball as it zoomed passed his foot.

'Ah, Tom!' came the grumbles of the others on his team.

He ignored them and started walking away.

'Alright?' James asked, as they came face to face, just out of earshot of the nattering women. James' mam didn't stick around like the rest. She did shifts at the hospital and would hop straight on the bus when he was safely delivered at the school's gates.

'Tired,' Tomas admitted. 'Weird dream. My head was hurting all morning.'

'Least we haven't got any early mornings for the next six weeks!' James pointed out.

Tomas smiled at him. James' cow-lick was extremely large today. The curl of his hair to the left of his forehead pointed towards the sky in an exaggerated flick, and no matter how many times James licked his hand to squash it flat, it sprung right back up again.

They'd become best friends quite quickly. James had noticed Tomas lived close by and had started making a point of visiting him on weekends. They'd sit on the overgrown front lawn of Tomas' house and talk about video games and Goosebumps books for hours. James had promised to bring a spud-gun one day, just as soon as he convinced his mam to buy one from the market.

'I reckon today will be easy.'

'You think?' Tomas asked. They began walking towards the door that was closest to their classroom. The boys on the football pitch seemed to be thinking the same thing, moving away in talkative groups.

'Yea, nice and easy. Teachers don't like working just as much as we don't.'

James' prediction wasn't far wrong. Their teacher, Mrs Locke, seemed content in letting them pull out sugar-paper sheets from the activity tray and draw for the best part of the day.

'Look at this,' James said, sliding his paper towards Tomas. There was a rough sketch of a house made of wood, balanced on a tree branch.

'Cool,' Tomas replied, looking down at the fire-breathing dragon he'd been sketching in red. The Welsh flag above Mrs Locke's white board had inspired him, but he'd added two sets of wings instead of one. He didn't want to be accused of copying.

'I was thinking see, this could be our summer project.'

Tomas' eyes widened in realisation. 'A treehouse?'

'Yeah! It would be amazing. Somewhere we can hide out and watch for intruders. I've got so many plans! We just need to find the right tree.'

'But wood? Nails? A hammer? Where would we get . . .'

'We'll figure that out,' James cut in, with a wave of dismissal. He had a vision and he wasn't going to let anyone stomp on it. 'So you wanna help me?'

Tomas looked at the sketch. He thought about the wonders of climbing a ladder, up into a leafy canopy and staring down at the world, out of reach. They could steal food from home – stuff that their mams wouldn't miss – and squirrel it away for the long days it would take to hammer each piece of wood lovingly into place. Maybe they could have two levels? A room each! They could even sleep in it one night if they played their cards right.

Tomas grinned from ear to ear. 'This is going to be awesome.'

Chapter Two

THE TREES looked like broccoli. That's what Tomas always thought when he looked at the mountains on either side of him. Being nestled in a valley made for a beautiful view. Opening the front door could take your very breath away if you weren't used to it. There was the smell of daffodils in early spring and the cries of the sheep on the hills during lambing season. The river Taff drew older kids in wellington boots with their fathers' fishing rods, and in the shallower parts of the water you could see the smaller fish chasing each other for interesting tit-bits. People sat on their doorsteps in the summer to bathe in the sun's rays and everyone in the valley seemed to know everyone else, with an 'Alright, butty?' and a wink or a wave.

The world seemed smaller in the valleys, like nobody could touch the people there as long as they had each other. Tomas often thought that was the main reason his mam had moved in the first place. For the peace it brought that a city couldn't offer.

'Right then, where shall we start?' James asked at the park. Tomas had been there for a little while already, watching a crow peck at an empty crisp packet from the swing he was sat on.

'Taff Trail,' Tomas suggested, jumping onto the concrete. His feet tingled unpleasantly from the force of the landing.

'My thoughts exactly!' James cheered.

The boys raced off, feeling giddy with possibility. The first day of the holiday had begun. It was time to do some *real men's* work.

They cut up to the trail along the back gardens of a row of terraced houses and surveyed the hills. There were plenty of trees, but most were tall with branches that were far too high for a couple of nine-year-olds. Slipping across farmers' fields to the trees on their outskirts, they carefully considered each one.

'We're getting too far away,' James mumbled, in a glum tone. 'It would take forever to drag the wood here.'

Doubling back, they took the trail in the opposite direction, running in spurts and then stopping to point at potential trees for their home away from home.

Then they saw it: low leafy branches, thick for feet to clamber over, and plenty of height to build a treehouse away from prying eyes. The tree itself was on a hill overlooking the community leisure centre that the school took them for swimming lessons. Tomas couldn't swim very well, so he didn't enjoy the trips to the pool as much as he probably should. The smell and occasional swallowing of chlorine gave him a bad belly afterwards. And he could never shake that fear of slipping into the deep end of the pool, where the water looked a darker shade of crystal.

'This is it,' James decided, with a sureness in his voice that made Tomas sure too. 'This is our tree.'

Tomas stood on one of the lower branches and tested its strength, putting all his weight on it and then bouncing up and down. James joined him and they laughed as the leaves shook a happy melody above them.

'Now what?' Tomas wondered.

'We get the wood.'

'But where from?'

James smiled a sneaky smile. 'Follow me.'

✳

At a house, not far from his own, Tomas looked up at the red and white FOR SALE sign nailed to its wall. At the back there was a garden, big and square, with a fence that had collapsed. The wood looked old and was a dirty, stained colour with bird poop in places – where they'd perched their bums and watched the world go by, letting the mess slither down with a chirruping cry of relief. Nevertheless, James was acting like he'd struck gold.

'We can drag these broken bits away. They're not heavy. I've tested them. They come away easily enough too. Watch . . .' He kicked at an upright piece of fencing and the nail that was supporting it seemed to pop out with no resistance.

'Let's take what we can and come back.'

Tomas glanced nervously around. He didn't like to steal. But if the house was FOR SALE, did that mean no one would mind? There weren't any people inside to spot him and complain, right?

He was about to tell James it was a bad idea when his mind suddenly filled with images of a tree swing, right up in the highest boughs, and a roof over their heads when storms hit. They could bring torches and tell scary stories to one another. He could even stash his Battleships board-game there for them to play, because they had both agreed one afternoon that it was by far the best non-video-game you could own. Better even than Connect Four.

Bending down, Tomas started pulling the wood into a neat-ish pile before lifting them to his chest. They were considerably lighter than he'd thought, but he hadn't anticipated the bite of splinters and loose nails.

James was carrying a pile twice as big as his, so Tomas behaved as if he wasn't finished yet – kicking a few planks away from their base and dragging them into his arms.

'Let's move quickly, in case someone stops us,' James instructed.

Tomas felt a twinge of panic. His mam didn't leave the house very often, but if she happened to see him, she'd pull her hair out.

Tomas overtook James in his fear of being caught and together they sped to their tree, dropping the wood next to the waving fronds of the ferns that grew in mass that time of year.

They returned to the house to gather more wood, and on their third visit, they became slightly more timid about the operation. There were kids in the park, circling on bikes and guffawing at badly executed stunts on some crumbly, old steps. Tomas and James realized that they had taken most of the loose planks, leaving a row of undamaged, firmly nailed ones to contend with.

'I think we should make do for now,' Tomas suggested feebly. 'We have plenty to start with, don't you think?'

James nodded in silent agreement.

'Hey, do you fancy getting a drink? I'm super thirsty,' he added.

'You can get it at mine if you want?' James said, forgetting about their mini predicament for the moment. 'Mam's in work. So is Dad. It's just my sister home. We can look for his toolbox while they're out. I haven't had the chance to because they've been home, see?'

'Come on then.' Tomas started jogging up the street towards the gully that led to his friend's house. At the far end of the hill, in a little terraced house, they pushed open the back gate and stampeded into the kitchen. James raided the fridge for cold cans of lemonade and they drained them thirst-quenchingly before either of them could speak again.

'Tools are under the stairs,' James informed, putting the empty, sweating can on the side. He looked at it for a heartbeat and then swept it into the recycling bin just outside the back door. 'Act normal,' he reminded Tomas.

Tomas followed him stealthily through the living room. They were soldiers on a mission: retrieve the tools and get them back to camp before the enemy could locate them.

They tried not to giggle as they ducked down low, slipping into the hallway and heading towards the shadows under the staircase.

'What are you two doing?' came a voice.

Eleri was standing by the front door with her mobile phone in one hand and half-eaten rocket lolly in the other. Her long blonde hair was tied back in a graceful ponytail and her ears were supporting big gold hoops.

'Nothin',' James shrugged. 'Playing.'

Eleri frowned as if she didn't believe them. Not for one minute. 'Yeah, well, Mam's finishing early. She's not feeling too good, so you better keep this house spotless or else she'll be annoyed with *both* of us, you hear me?'

'I'm going back out anyway,' James said, ignoring the warning tone in her voice.

'Well, you've only got half-hour left before you've gotta come in.'

Tomas made a face of bemusement. Was it that late already? They had been backwards and forwards over the hills looking around for hours and the wood-stocking operation had taken a while. Eleri was probably right. Time was getting on.

She sloped away into the living room and closed the door with one last look of suspicion at her little brother. When she was gone, James pounced on the toolbox he knew was tucked out of sight.

'Look. It's got everything we need. Hammer. Nails. Screws. Erm . . .' he picked up a tool he couldn't identify and dropped it back into the box with a clunk. 'Tape measure.'

'Is there a grappling hook?' Tomas wondered eagerly. He'd heard the word on

Batman and wasn't sure if men used them on a regular basis, at building sites perhaps?

'No, but there's a little saw!' James waved the saw in front of Tomas' eyes.

'We can't take the whole box though, surely? It's way too heavy.'

James pondered this for a minute. 'I'll take what I can tomorrow. Meet you at the tree, yeah?'

'Sure.'

'I might as well stay in now. Eleri will only grass me up if I'm back late. Half an hour is, like, *nothing*. By time I walk to the park it'll be time to come in.'

Tomas understood and bid his friend goodbye.

In the morning, construction would begin on possibly the bestest, coolest thing they'd ever EVER done.

Chapter Three

HE TOOK his seat and selected a pencil, already eager for break-time to come. He had an apple in his school bag that his mam had given him and was imagining the sweet juices in his mouth – his teeth crunching down on grainy flesh to fill his aching belly.

Gosh, he was hungry. The porridge that morning had been gloopier than usual and to add to the nightmare, there had been no sugar left. He liked his porridge sugary. Mam always sprinkled one small spoonful on the top before she served him his bowl, but sometimes, when she was busy and unaware, he'd rush over for more.

'Anthony? Your chair is on my workbook,' came a voice that stirred his hungry thoughts.

He looked at the girl next to him and then down at the dusty floor. He had been so absorbed in thoughts of eating something tasty that he hadn't even noticed the difference in balance on the one side of his seat.

'Oh! Sorry. Here you go . . .' He slid the chair back and picked the book up. There were dirt marks where the chair's legs had pressed into it. Hurriedly, he brushed it clean and handed it over.

She smiled nervously as she accepted it and then turned to the front of the class, already delving into the equations teacher was putting on the black board to solve.

Anthony's eyes lingered on the girl for a moment and then flitted to the window that

was creating a halo of light around her and
his classmates' heads. It was still murky out,
but the sun was fighting to come through.

His stomach rumbled.

Then the world rumbled too.

*

Tomas' head whipped up from his pillow
as his room came alive with a bright white
light. Thunder followed, grumbling across the
valley and sending lashes of rain against the
Merthyr rooftops.

How could this be happening? No wonder
he'd been dreaming about strange rumbling
sounds! His peaceful, warm, summer night
had been torn apart with a storm that
threatened all his dreams and plans for the
incoming day.

'Argh, n-o-o-o!' he growled, yanking his
duvet off and walking to the window. Even
the lamp-post opposite was swaying slightly

in the wind, illuminating the fat raindrops as they barreled down at a slant.

Tomas crawled back into bed, miserable. If the rain didn't stop, his mam would keep him from hanging out with James at their special, chosen tree.

Why'd it have to rain?

But by the morning, the downpour had become a drizzle and Tomas was up early, having felt the rumbling of hunger in his belly all night. He fixed his cereal and perched on a chair at the table, watching the soggy clothes drip-drip-dripping outside on the washing line.

Mam didn't stop him from going out. She seemed preoccupied with her mobile phone and also showed signs of a smile. Tomas blinked rapidly as she ran her hands through his hair on passing, and stared after her as she hummed a random tune. Something strange was afoot.

Tomas was the first to arrive at the tree,

but James was quick to join him. His friend lumbered along with a Tesco Bag for Life, upending it on the ground to show what he'd managed to pinch.

'We've got enough to start,' he said, running his fingers through the pile of semi-rusty nails. 'Make every one count!'

'Let's do the ladder first then,' Tomas suggested, reaching for a hammer. There were two of them in the pile. One was slightly smaller and a whole lot lighter than the other. He took the heavier hammer and slipped it into his belt, like Batman would with *his* tools.

'Longest pieces I can find,' James announced, dropping two planks. He reached for his Tesco bag and found the little saw still hiding in the bottom. 'I'll cut smaller pieces for the steps and you can hammer them in.'

They set to work, cutting and positioning, nailing and examining their work. It took James a while to get enough steps cut, but when they were done, the ladder looked glorious.

'Lift it!' Tomas said, looking to James for support. They both picked the structure up and carried it to the tree trunk – which was slick with rain – but because of the tree's many branches, it wouldn't lean flat. 'That branch is sticking out.'

'I'm on it!' James said, retrieving his saw and hacking away at the branch.

It was tiresome work and Tomas was getting irritable as he stood idly by, feeling the drippers of rainwater in the leaves tumbling down his neck every now and again. When James had chopped off enough of the branch, they lifted the ladder back into place and set to work nailing it to the tree.

'These nails are too short,' Tomas complained. 'I keep hammering them in but they pop back out again. The ladder isn't very sturdy.' He rocked the ladder in demonstration and it slid off the tree with ease.

'Hmmm,' James mumbled in annoyance. 'I'll have to find some longer ones at home, I guess.'

Tomas sighed as they placed the ladder flat. So far, the day was proving a disaster. Nothing was working as he'd hoped it would. But he wasn't going to give up.

'Let's just hide the ladder in the ferns and go to the park. I can't be bothered to go home now. Mam's sick and she's let the birds out. They're flying all around the house, chirping and flapping in my face all the time. She says it cheers her up to see them free, though.'

Tomas helped cover the ladder and the tools with leafy fronds and then wiped the moist, grubby palms of his hands against his jeans. He felt a stirring of concern inside that no matter how well he hid the ladder, someone would steal it for their own.

'Can you see it from the trail?' Tomas asked.

'Nah, it's all good and hidden.'

At the park, the swings had been taken over by teenagers. Their long legs dangled lifelessly and their hands held the chains with limp wrists – having no intention of swinging whatsoever. Tomas scowled at them as he and James wandered through the gate and eyed up someplace else to haunt.

'Baby swings?'

'Wet,' James pointed out. The black rubber held little pools of water. 'I've got a better idea anyway. Cops and robbers.'

Tomas smiled. He liked a good game of cops and robbers – though it was usually more thrilling with a group of people, instead of just two.

'I'm going to hide in the memorial gardens. Rules are: street is off-limits, but you can use the park though, if you want. Catch me, then we swap. Deal?'

Tomas nodded enthusiastically.

'Count to fifty!' James yelled, as he ran back through the gate.

Tomas got to thirty-five before he lost patience. He ducked out of the gate and slipped into the memorial gardens like a leopard slinking through tall grass. There were plenty of vibrant plants growing and a multitude of walls to hide around. Tomas pressed his back against one wall and peeked around it with a rising giggle. Adrenaline kicked in and he imagined he had a gun at his hip and a team at his back, ready to take James out.

A twig snapped.

Tomas' ears picked up the sound and he sprinted as soundlessly as he could along the path. He spotted James cutting across the gardens in the distance, sliding in the wet grass and laughing.

Tomas changed direction, darting around a wall to head him off. He nearly trod in the flower patch, but caught himself just in time. Hopping over, he gained some ground and tried to reach for James' arm . . .

'Oi!'

A bark from the other side of the fence caught Tomas off guard and he froze. James, on the other hand, saw his chance and ran out of sight.

'Get out of there if you're going to play games. Have some bleedin' respect!'

Tomas' cheeks flared the red of ripe strawberries. His skin burned all over. The groundskeeper approached the green metal fencing that surrounded the gardens from the road. He'd left a wheelbarrow on the pavement that appeared to be full of fresh compost.

'Are you listening?' he shouted. 'Sling your hook!'

Riddled in guilt, Tomas traipsed off in pursuit of the exit, hoping James had had the sense to leave when the groundskeeper's voice had first sliced through their game.

As Tomas followed the path leading out, he saw James in the distance, standing under a tree that was shivering in the breeze.

'We've gotta go,' he hissed at him.

He remained in the dappled light, with the jewel like drops of rain on the leaves plopping all around him.

'James!' Tomas snapped, feeling the eyes of the groundskeeper on them, his embarrassment creeping like cold fingers up his back.

'What you yelling for?' came a call from beyond the exit.

Tomas turned and his eyes landed on his friend waiting for him. Confused, he looked back at the tree. But whoever had been standing there was gone.

Chapter Four

TOMAS WENT home feeling incredibly tired. The damp in his clothes from playing around the sopping wet trees had set into his skin. He was just about ready to nod off in the bathtub, but shook his head until the dream dust slipped away from the corners of his thoughts. When he was all dried off and wearing his blue-striped pyjamas, he plodded downstairs on sleepy feet to find his mam in the kitchen frying bacon and eggs.

'A cooked breakfast? In the night?' he asked her, incredulous. She was a firm believer of vegetables and fruit. She tried to eat healthy and avoided greasy foods, which meant Tomas had to as well.

'I fancied something naughty. And I couldn't afford a takeaway, so I've done the next best thing.'

Tomas' plate was piled high with slices of toast, mushrooms, tomatoes, bacon and two glistening eggs; their yummy middles unbroken and ready to be burst. He dipped the edge of his bread into the yellow dome and watched the yolk avalanche thickly over the sides. Not a crumb was left uneaten.

'Good?' his mam asked him. She'd had one less egg than him, but had still devoured the lot. He'd never seen her enjoy a meal so much.

He nodded. *Really* good. Thanks!' He made to take the dirty plates, to show how grateful he was for the treat, but his mam was already up and away with them.

With nothing left to do, he hopped off his chair and went in pursuit of a book he could tuck into, but his mam called out his name.

He paused in the doorway.

'I . . . I've arranged for you to sleep over James' house tomorrow night,' she said, leaning against the counter. 'Mammy's . . . well . . . she's going out. Is that okay?'

Tomas stared at her. Why wouldn't it be okay? She'd barely been anywhere, besides the cafe with Samantha since his dad had left them when he was four. He'd had to endure the tears through the walls at night as she'd cried his dad's name and suffer the sad feelings of his own, brimming and spilling inside him when he was alone sometimes.

'Are you going with Sam?'

She hesitated. 'Yes . . . Sam will be there.' She turned to the cupboard and pulled out a chocolate bar, which she tossed his way. He caught it with a snap and smiled. Crunchie. His favourite.

'Don't let any crumbs melt in your bed,' she warned.

'I won't!' he promised, already tearing into it.

*

That night, there were no confusing dreams of rumbling and of people he'd never seen before. Tomas woke feeling full of energy, and managed to get to his tree far earlier than any other day.

Without James around, he eagerly climbed the branches – slats of wood in hand – having breathed a sigh of utmost relief when he'd discovered their ladder was still safely hidden and intact.

By the time James arrived, Tomas had already managed to lay most of the base. It wasn't perfectly straight because the higgledy-piggledy branches made it impossible, but it was flat enough to sit and stand on quite comfortably.

'My mam made me clean my room,' James grumbled, as he joined Tomas on their new wooden base in the leaves above. 'Sorry I'm late. But, wow! You've really done a lot!'

Tomas wiped sweat from his forehead. 'Yeah. But we've run out of good wood.'

At the base of the tree were little off-cuts from the steps they'd made. Nothing worthy of using for their walls.

'We need to go hunting again,' James realised.

'Any ideas where?'

They thought about it *really* hard.

'The skip?' James suggested suddenly.

'Too many people around,' Tomas pointed out. There were always people in cars dumping rubbish and one of them could possibly be a parent from his school. If they told on him, he'd have to explain to his mam why he'd been rifling through dirty bins.

'We could just wander for scraps. There's always scraps in the village.'

Tomas shrugged casually. 'Cool. Sure.'

'Oooooor . . .' James sang, 'we could start making the treehouse's booby traps!'

Tomas grinned mischievously. 'To stop people taking over?'

'I was thinking about it last night. My dad's left his shovel in the garden. We could dig a hole just here,' he pointed at the soft, grassy earth, 'and fill it with dog poo.'

Tomas looked bewildered for a moment. Then, he envisioned a nasty brute heckling them from the Taff Trail – trying to invade and conquer, only to tumble into a pit of poo. That would *surely* scare them off from any future trickery.

He felt a giggle bubbling inside. 'We'd be the only ones who know to jump over!'

'Exactly,' James sniggered wickedly.

Together, they dashed to pick up the shovel from James' garden and in the afternoon heat, James dug a hole. Tomas was given the foul but necessary duty of locating dog mess.

He had a bag and a stick, which he used to prod his trophy finds, before squishing them into the carrier and moving onto the next. Luckily for them, the Taff Trail was full of dog walkers whose pets had active bums.

Tomas tipped the mess into the shallow pit, wishing he had a peg for his nose. Some of the mess was still gloopy and it stuck to the insides of the bag, until he shook it hard.

'Perfect!' James celebrated, dropping the shovel. 'The smell alone should scare off our enemies.'

They climbed the ladder to their new treehouse base and sat with their legs dangling over the edge, staring at the blue sky that peeked through the leaves above. Tomas knew his friend was thinking the same as him – hoping against hope that someone would show up and test their booby trap.

The trail was vacant, probably because

lunchtime had snuck up and made bellies feel empty, but Tomas spotted a shadow in the distance that couldn't be mistaken.

'Intruder alert! Intruder alert!' he announced, in a deep voice.

'Where?' James cried, turning his head this way and that.

Tomas lowered his tone to a secretive one. 'By the horse field. At the gate. There's a boy standing there. Look! He's spotted our treehouse. He wants to attack!'

'I don't see anyone,' James moaned. 'Where?'

'The gate. By the horse field. Look between these branches.' He pressed his hands against two of the bigger boughs that their wooden planks were nailed to. 'You can see him right there!' Tomas tried not to speak too loudly, or else he'd give away their position amongst the greenery. He wished he'd thought to wear camouflage, or even something distinctly tree-coloured.

'That's just a horse,' James said matter-of-factly, as if his friend was behaving stupidly.

Tomas' mouth gaped open and he spluttered for a moment, thinking of the words to say. The boy in the distance was standing right there! Looking at their tree!

'You need to go to Specsavers,' Tomas concluded, watching the figure like a hawk would watch a mouse. The boy wasn't threatening them in any way. He seemed to be alone. When he'd stared at Tomas long enough, he returned to petting the horse that was feeding on the tall grass.

'Mam said I'm due an eye exam,' James admitted. 'But I really don't want to go, just in case they make me wear glasses. I hate them.'

'Harry Potter wears glasses. He's cool.'

James shrugged. 'So does my dad, and he looks like a scientist. But do you see Batman wearing them? Or Wolverine? No. And I want to be strong like them.'

'Superman does, though. When he's pretending to be normal. And I think Spiderman wears them sometimes, when he's not swinging between buildings, I mean.'

'I guess so,' James said. He appeared to be bored of the glasses debate. Tomas could tell by the tone of his voice.

Instead of superheroes in specs, Tomas started to think about their treehouse building progress: all the wood they'd lugged up hills and all the hammering and assembling they'd done for the past couple of days. 'I think we're pretty strong, like someone in a comic book. We've made this so far, haven't we, just based on a sketch you did at school.'

'You could say that, yea.' James perked up. He looked in the direction of the horse field. 'Hey, is he still there? The enemy?'

Tomas shot a look over – in warrior-scout mode again, pretending his hands were binoculars – but there was no one present, besides the hairy steed hungering for plants.

*

Eleri was babysitting. As it turned out, James' mam and dad were going to the cinema and then for a meal, so the boys had the television to themselves to play video games. Eleri was in the living room with them, sprawled on her dad's computer chair and tapping away at the keyboard. She had a glass of something fruity that she drank with a straw. When James had asked to try some, she'd told him to get lost.

'Cow,' he muttered.

'Moose,' she replied, sucking on the pink straw so hard it made slurp noises to make him jealous.

'Anyway, you're getting fat,' James spat at her. 'Even Mam noticed!'

Tomas had been enthralled by the zombie

game James had put on, but he felt somewhat distracted now that there was sibling banter bouncing backwards and forwards across the room. He didn't have the privilege at home. He'd always wanted a brother or sister, but Mam had said she couldn't afford another baby – plus she liked giving her time and energy to him alone. At least, that's what she told him.

'You'd better shut your trap, boyo. I heard you and Spiderman over there were playing up in the memorial gardens the other day.'

James blanched. 'We were playing cops and robbers. So what? And how do *you* know?'

She put her drink down. 'My mate happened to drive by and she saw you in there larking around. It's not funny you know. That place is like, sacred.'

Tomas looked at James, feeling his cheeks burning. He should have known it was a bad idea chasing each other in there.

There were gates and grumpy gardeners for a reason.

'It's just some fancy garden,' James bit back.

'Wrong! It's a MEMORIAL garden, moron. That's where a school got crushed and a load of kids got killed. Read the sign on the wall, or don't they teach you how in school anymore?'

'What happened to them?' Tomas croaked unexpectedly. He had died in the game he was playing – zombies chewing at his face – because he'd forgotten to press pause. The game was of no interest to him anymore.

Eleri turned to her computer. She started tapping away. 'Here we are. Look. The Aberfan Disaster. A landslide came down. Killed 116 children and 28 adults.'

Tomas felt sick all of a sudden. His stomach lurched and his brow prickled.

'It happened on the twenty-first of October, 1966. You probably won't remember it because you were babies, but the Queen came just to plant something in the garden. Everyone was standing in the centre park and all along the roads to wave at her. We got a day off school. It was great.'

Their argument forgotten now, James joined his sister at the computer and leaned over her shoulder to look at the screen. Tomas wandered over too, feeling slightly shaken and timid. How could he have run around such a special place? No wonder the groundskeeper was furious!

On the screen there was a black and white picture of people with shovels digging in the mud. A young boy in a hat was standing by, overlooking the sad reality. Some houses looked crushed. Tomas recognised the street. He'd run up and down Moy Road many times to go to the shops and buy sweets from Trevor's.

'They say the village was deadly silent after. So many kids had died, and so many people's lives were hit by the tragedy. It's so sad. Could you imagine?'

Tomas swallowed the lump in his throat. He didn't want to imagine.

Eleri's phone buzzed on the desk and she plucked it up, smiling at whatever had been sent. Her fingers danced over the buttons in response, almost a blur.

James was already away, picking up the game controller and tapping at the buttons to reset it. 'Let's play two players,' he decided, immersing himself in the plush red cushions spread across the floor.

'It's okay. I'll just watch,' Tomas replied. For some reason, he just didn't feel like it.

Chapter Five

THE RUMBLING was the only thing anyone could hear. Anthony and his classmates looked to one another in a mixture of sudden fear and puzzlement. The pencil on his desk rolled to the floor. His teacher was no longer facing the blackboard but the window.

Where was it coming from? Above them? Below? Was it a helicopter? An earthquake? Stampeding cows or horses?

He was aware of his own heavy breathing.

The fog was still resting on the mountain-side in curling, swirling masses; and from its grey heart there suddenly came an extraordinarily terrifying sight . . .

A black wave of muck was rampaging towards them, dragging boulders out from the soil, swallowing telegraph poles and ripping up trees.

It moved so fast, Anthony could barely get to his feet before it . . .

*

'NO!' Tomas yelled in the dark. It took him a few sharp breaths to realise where he was and why he had screamed.

'You all right?' James whispered from their nest of cushions and blankets. They'd decided to sleep in the living room after watching a scary film that had been forbidden to them – on pain of death by Eleri. It had taken Tomas' mind off the memorial gardens stunt at first. There had been so much violence and gore in the story, he hadn't known where to look.

'Yea. Sorry to wake you. I thought I felt something run up my arm,' he lied – because thinking it could have been a spider was a whole heap easier to explain than what he'd *actually* been dreaming about.

The birds in the corner of the living room were ruffling and flapping around in their cages, alarmed by the disturbance. Parrots and parakeets were James' mam's favourite things in the world. James had said on numerous occasions: he thought she liked them more than him.

'Probably shouldn't have watched that film, mate.'

'It *was* pretty messed up,' Tomas agreed. He had enjoyed it, but he'd had to remind himself over and over it wasn't real. None of it. Just sickening make-up and close up camera angles to make you feel like you were a part of the horror. If he could go back, he'd suggest they just watch *Terminator* instead, as he was quite fond of Arnie films.

'Next time you stay over, we'll watch another one. Think how cool we'll be when we go back to school and can actually discuss horror films with the boys for a change!'

'Definitely,' Thomas murmured with a yawn.

He lay in the dark staring at the ceiling. He wished deep down that Eleri hadn't told him about the disaster in 1966. His mind was flooded with thoughts of what the village must have been like in the aftermath. So sad. So quiet. He started to wonder if there were any survivors still alive, or people who had been around when it happened – perhaps still in the village?

'My torch is here if you need to check for that spider,' James assured him, placing it above Tomas' head. 'Just think, though, if you get bitten you might have super powers.'

Tomas smiled at this.

In the morning, James' mam insisted on driving Tomas home, even though he only lived around the corner. He'd filled up on coco pops before he'd bundled his belongings in the car and promised James he'd see him later. Usual, secret place.

He felt uncomfortable in the car. It wasn't often he got to sit in one, because his mam couldn't drive. A handful of times they'd caught the train back to Cardiff, which had been his biggest adventure as far as transport went. She'd take him to Primark two to three times a year to stock up on pants and socks, amongst other things. Now that they didn't live in the city, it was harder lugging all the shopping bags home.

'Going anywhere nice with your mam this year?'

The question made him flush with nervous heat. 'No. Not really. Mam's looking for a job.'

'Ah, I see,' she said, in a tone that suggested she had already expected that answer. 'Well never mind, eh? I'm sure you and my boy are having lots of fun out and about. It's nice to be free from homework for a bit, I bet?'

'I have some work to do,' he said, 'but we've got ages yet.'

She nodded as she pulled the car up outside Tomas' house. As he opened the car door, the front door to his home opened and his mam stood there waving.

'Did you have fun?' she called from the doorstep.

Tomas nodded as he grabbed his bags from the boot.

'Good night, Carys?' James' mam asked her. She'd rolled the window down so she could holler out.

'Very good. Thanks.'

'Well, anytime. You know that. Tomas is always welcome!'

'Cheers, Leanne.'

They waved the car off and slipped inside the house. Tomas dumped his bag on the bottom step, receiving a frown from his mam and a quick reminder that bags didn't belong there. He popped it upstairs and returned with the dirty washing, finding his mam in the kitchen on her phone. Her thumbs were moving feverishly over the keys and her dimples were showing. It reminded him of Eleri the night before.

'Here you go,' he said, looking for approval as he brandished his pile of dirty washing.

'Put it in the basket,' she instructed, still looking down at the tiny mobile screen. Her phone was still brick shaped with an aerial poking from the top. If the adverts were anything to go by, she was behind with upgrades.

'I'm going out, okay?' he told her, whilst slam-dunking his clothes into the wicker basket near the back door.

'Have you eaten?'

'Yup.'

'Okay. Be careful.'

'I wiiiiiiill,' he insisted on his way out.

His magnificent tree was waving as he approached – the branches shimmering in the sunlight. He suddenly felt all his previous worries slide right off him and a smile touched his lips as he sprinted towards the ladder.

There was nothing he could do now but wait. A wood-gathering expedition still needed to be arranged and possibly a quest for more nails. Their little stash had dwindled and only the scabby, slightly bent ones remained.

As he perched on the uneven base of his treehouse – considering getting rope and a sturdy twig for a swing – noises sounded on the trail nearby. Ducking, he made himself as small as possible in the branches, peeking through at a mishmash of colours ahead.

Three teenage boys in bright patterned T-shirts and blue tracksuit bottoms were strolling by. One had a cigarette in hand that was leaving a lazy smoke trail. They were speaking loudly amongst themselves and cackling with laughter, until one of them spotted something interesting: the pit of dog mess.

'That's buzzing,' complained a boy in a dusty black cap with 'No Fear' stitched on the front in white.

'Look, look.' Another lad slapped his mate on the shoulder.

The three of them peered up at Tomas, who was crouching down with his back to them, trying his best to pretend they weren't there. If James had been around, they would have played the part of soldiers protecting what was rightfully theirs. But alone, he just didn't feel as brave.

'Sad,' one of the boys declared.

They moved on at last, leaving Tomas to heave a great big sigh of relief.

*

In the days that followed, Tomas and James managed to forage for rubbish wood all over the village. There were plenty of overflowing skips around, bearing interesting pieces of scrap, and it wasn't long before they'd gathered enough pieces of wood to start making their walls.

James had wanted to steal an old door that was propped up in an alley, but they'd struggled to lift it between them. He'd had high hopes of using it as their roof; imagining building a harness to lift it into the treetop and lower it down into place. But dreams were all they were allowed to be, and in the end they left the door face down and forgotten on the concrete.

'It's coming along great, isn't it?' James enthused, patting the planks like he was fussing over a beloved dog.

They'd grown impatient. The walls weren't high enough for them to stand when the roof was complete. With whispers of more rain heading their way, it felt like a race against time to get the treehouse finished, so they could plot and scheme and play without any eyes fixed on them.

Tomas had solved their 'nail' problem with a good rummage through the old shed in his garden. His mam had forbidden him to *ever* go inside because it was full of old junk belonging to the previous owner. But on a day when she seemed the most distracted, he'd crept into the cobwebbed darkness and found himself a pile of useful hardware, which he stashed in his jeans pockets.

'OUCH!' Tomas yelped. He'd missed the nail and struck his hand with the hammer.

'Oof. That'll bruise,' James concluded, with a quick glance. He was holding the plank steady for Tomas and generally keeping a close eye out for intruders.

'I think I broke my wrist,' he hissed.

'Like my mam always says, you'd know if you broke it. Look, it's moving fine.'

Tomas grumbled; twisting his hand this way and that, before reluctantly picking his

64

hammer back up. He realised as time wore on that James' mam was probably right – he'd know if he'd snapped his bone – although he did have a small bump rising on his skin that looked positively *nasty*.

Before the day was through, they'd secured their roof. Victorious and tired, the boys sat hunched inside, the tops of their heads brushing the ceiling. Neither of them wanted to admit the treehouse was nothing like they'd imagined it would be. Still, it was what it was. And best of all, it was theirs.

'Do you think people get bills if they live in a treehouse?'

'I don't know,' James replied, trying to pick a splinter from his thumb, with his tongue poking out in concentration. 'It's no different to a tramp sleeping in a box, right? And he has no money.'

'I'd love to live in the trees,' Tomas said dreamily.

'But you wouldn't be able to play video games in here.'

'I'd read books. Keep a torch here. Or candles even!'

'You're like a Victorian,' James said, 'in olden times. You'll be building a time machine next.'

Tomas grinned and thought about this. Yes, he'd love a time machine. He'd never live in the 'now'. He'd keep moving. He'd sample food all over the world and in different centuries. He'd try and find Jesus to see his miracles for real. He'd follow carnivals and circuses, where lion tamers and clowns travelled to sleepy towns. He'd try and be a hero, stopping all kinds of disasters –

His thoughts froze. Sure, if he had a time machine . . . he could warn people. He'd be some sort of dark messenger. He could spread the word about all kinds of events and save a whole bunch of people. Especially kids that needed rescuing.

'I think I'm done for the day,' he said quietly. 'I'm going to head home.'

'Me too. We can keep the tools here for a bit longer, just in case we need to make improvements.'

Tomas climbed down the ladder after James had his two feet securely on the ground. As part of their usual routine, they hid the tools in the tall grass and then hopped over their pit of dog poo. But before Tomas scurried on home, he looked up at the mountainside. It was covered in little white specks where the sheep were wandering and grazing. Serene and beautiful.

As it should be.

Chapter Six

TOMAS WAS actually standing there this time – as himself – watching the frenzied terror of the villagers as they tried to dig for survivors.

It didn't look real.

It just wasn't right, somehow. Like his brain was trying to force the image to blur into something else. Something less tragic.

People without shovels were using their hands, pulling bits of debris away. The desperation on their faces was frightening. Contagious.

More and more arrived on the scene to help.

More and more dirt was shifted.

More and more were found – unmoving.

*

Tomas woke with sweat all over his skin. His pyjamas were sticking to his back and his hair felt oily. He wished the nightmares would stop. He wished he could go to sleep and fall into an undisturbed, black nothingness. With each coming night, he was starting to dread his bed time.

Shaking off feelings of misery, he picked up his book from the bedside table. *The Twits*. He liked Roald Dahl books because no matter how grim the story, something magical and amazing would happen to put a smile on his face. It wasn't a very long book, and being a third of the way through already, he managed to finish it before he nodded off again.

This time, his sleep was dreamless.

*

'You can't go straight out to play today,' Mam said, as Tomas was munching his way through a snapping and crackling bowl of Rice Krispies. He looked mortified in response. 'I thought we could go see a film? What do you think?'

He swallowed. 'Can James come?'

Her cheeks bloomed red as she joined him at the table, sinking into the chair opposite. The kettle was starting to bubble and steam as it came to its end, making it difficult to hear each other. 'Oh, Tommy. I wish he could, but Mammy can't afford to bring friends.'

Tomas hated when she used words like *Mammy and Tommy*. He wasn't a baby anymore. He'd built his very own treehouse, for crying out loud! A treehouse that he very much wanted to check on . . .

'We could go into town for a bit and get you a new coat, too.'

He shrugged in defeat, knowing in his heart he would never win. 'Alright. Fine.'

Within the hour, they were standing at a blue bus stop with an elderly lady who, even in the heat of the summer, was dressed in a thick, cream coat. On the road, a sheepdog was risking life and limb to chase cars. There was no one around to claim the poor beast – which undoubtedly meant it had escaped – and with each passing car, it tried to nip at the wheels.

'Oh gosh,' his mam wheezed, with a hand over her mouth. Her look of concern fell upon Tomas, but he was staring ahead at the dog, slack-jawed.

'Why's it doing that?' he asked edgily.

His mam watched the dog as she spoke again, wincing. 'Collies are supposed to be known for this. Some sort of lunge mechanism. Your Auntie Jane had one years ago, before you were born. It tried chasing a quad bike on a walk and got hit. She was so upset.'

Tomas' eyes widened. That was *all* he

needed to hear. He'd be having nightmares about dogs under cars next!

The relief on his mam's face was clear as crystal when the bus pulled up, but Tomas feared what he might see on their return journey. At least for the time being, he could forget and enjoy himself.

*

Tomas ate too much warm toffee-coated popcorn and drank too much Coke – immersed in the fantastical colours of a 3-D film at the cinema. He laughed when his mam turned to him in her giant black glasses, poking her tongue out. Together they ignored the world's worries for a few hours of their lives.

They left the theatre feeling dazzled by the bright sunlight bouncing off the white slabs. The heat took them aback and Tomas' mam lifted her face to the sky for a moment before leading him into town.

There weren't a lot of clothes shops left in Merthyr. All the big colourful businesses had sad signs of closure. Lots of places declared SALE SALE SALE, but they were selling girlie dresses and high heeled shoes that looked impossible to stand in. Tomas had never seen his mam wearing anything that ridiculous. She was sensible, that's how *she* put it.

The main high street was full of bustling people of all shapes and sizes. Most had shorts and T-shirts on, flashing tattoos on arms, shoulders and in some cases, necks! He tried to think of a superhero he liked that had a tattoo, but couldn't quite remember any. Perhaps the ink dissolved under their skin? Or perhaps it made them sick? Either way, they were all inkless and pure.

His mam led him into a shop full of odds and ends. It was very random, with teacups here and old books there. There were framed pictures hanging in every direction and clothes racks all along the walls.

'You just need something to tide you over until winter. I'll get you a nice coat then, I promise.'

Tomas' eyes followed her around the shop. If she was planning on getting him a nice coat in the winter, did that mean she would be getting him a horrible one now? He hoped not. Dreading her approach, she held a jacket up, greeny-brown in colour. It had four big pockets on the front and a bronze-coloured zip.

'What do you think?'

He thought of his life among the leaves and branches and instantly beamed at her. 'Yes!'

She flinched in surprise. 'Really? Well, that was easy.'

When they were all paid up, she allowed Tomas to carry the shopping bag. 'We've got bad weather coming next week, so don't just dump this at the bottom of your wardrobe, okay?'

'I won't,' he promised.

As they headed towards the bus stop, Tomas' mam stopped in her tracks. He followed her gaze to a man standing by a lamp-post, holding a lead. The lead was attached to a big black dog.

'Oh, shoot. I forgot bread,' she said quickly.

Tomas frowned. 'I can get it for you when we get home if you –'

'No. I need it now,' she insisted, turning swiftly.

'Carys?'

A voice sounded behind them. Tomas' mam fixed a smile on her lips and turned.

'Heya, Daniel. Nice surprise.'

He came over with his dog in tow, his blonde hair swept back with gel and his eyes a piercing blue. He was skinny for a man, Tomas thought. And he looked like a happy soul. On his bicep there was a tattoo of a wolf, shaded in black, grey and white.

'So, is this the little man?' he wondered, with a sneaky wink.

She nodded sheepishly. 'Yea . . . Yes . . . ! This is my son.' She put a hand on his back for encouragement.

'All right there, Tomas?' the man asked, patting him on the head.

Tomas was speechless. If the stranger knew his name already, he probably knew his mam, somehow . . .

'I'll speak to you later, Daniel,' his mam promised with a hint of firmness. 'We've got to catch the bus, sorry.'

Daniel stood to his full height, which was rather staggering. He towered over them both. The dog snuffled Tomas' shoes and gave a whiney yawn that distracted Tomas briefly.

'Oh. Right. Sure.' Daniel backed away casually, almost stumbling over a crack in the slabs. 'Nice seeing you, Carys. And you, Tomas.'

Tomas had buttoned his lips. Funnily enough, he didn't feel the same way.

*

When Tomas hopped off the bus, he gave a cautionary look left and right, and felt a wave of weightless joy ripple through him when he spotted the sheepdog lying by the curb with his tail wagging. He was calm now, and his eyes weren't drawn by the whirling, whistling wheels of the cars that tore by. Next to the dog, there sat a boy. He had dark hair and pale skin. His hand was gently gliding over the dog's back, starting from his furry neck and slipping over the glossy hairs to the tip of the dog's wagging tail.

'He's calmed down, at least,' Tomas' mam pointed out, as she checked her bag for her belongings (as she always did after jumping off the bus) and started walking away.

'Yea,' Tomas agreed, finding himself

staring more at the boy than the dog. It seemed odd that he couldn't place the boy's face. He looked to be about his age. Most of the children in the village went to Tomas' school, besides a select few . . . but he'd seen those kids in the park, or at the shops. This boy was new. He was sure of it.

'Tomas, come on! I want to get dinner done,' his mam scolded. She was already a good distance ahead.

He jolted and followed, stuffing his hands in the pockets of his jeans in thought.

Chapter Seven

'SO WHO was that man in town?' Tomas asked, as they sat at the dinner table eating a tuna pasta bake, with crunched up crisps and cheddar cheese on the top. The cheese came away with his fork in stringy lines that he played with before eating.

He hadn't gone out to play after his adventure to the cinema. It was getting too late to really plan anything, and although the popcorn had filled him up hours ago, he had a rumbly belly again and a desire to watch his mam cooking.

In the kitchen, he'd sat and doodled in

his sketch book. He liked to draw. He was getting pretty good. At least his teacher had said so.

'Who?' his mam said, not looking up from her plate.

Tomas detected her nervous posture. 'That man with the dog.'

'He's Samantha's friend.'

'Oh. Right.' He chewed slowly for a moment before speaking again. 'You told him about me, though?'

She finally looked at him. 'Of course I did, Tomas. You're the best thing I ever made.'

Tomas thought this was a weird thing to say. How on earth had she made him? Did she glue his eyes and ears on? If that was the case, she could have made his ears stick out less. And James' mam could have avoided making that horrid cow-lick with his fringe, too.

'What's his dog's name?'

'Um . . . Betty. No wait, Bessie. That's it.'

She poked at the pasta on her plate. Her phone was next to her glass of orange juice, which was strange. She'd never been particularly bothered about it being near her at all times, until recently.

The conversation went flat and Tomas got bored. He finished his pasta – leaving the offending sweetcorn pieces all over his plate like wounded men in a tomato fight – and took his sketch book to the bedroom.

He finished his picture by lamplight – an image of himself with a pirate patch over one eye and cutlass in hand, swinging from the branch of his secret tree. The treehouse was there, looking considerably better than the real thing. And James was sitting on a swing, which they had yet to make in real life.

As he stared at his finished masterpiece, he smiled. The feelings of merriment that brimmed inside him came naturally when he thought about his life.

Reaching to turn the page of his sketch

book, he halted abruptly. A shadow had fallen over the page, like an eclipse.

Gasping, he swivelled on his chair.

But the room was empty.

*

'So where did you go yesterday?' James asked, as Tomas took a running leap over the poo-pit. It was dry enough to go out, but the sky was muggy with the threat of a storm and he'd been warned by his mam: first sign of a downpour – come *home*!

'We saw the new *X-Men* film. In 3-D. It was class.'

'Oh, really? Wow. Wish I could have seen it. But Dad always just buys copies off someone in work that still have, like, *lines* all over the screen where the actors are on ropes and that. It's rubbish.'

'I asked my mam for you, but she couldn't afford it.'

'It's okay. I came here for a bit to wait for you, then went back and completed Resident Evil on the Playstation.'

Tomas tapped on the wooden planks and inspected the corners of the treehouse. There were no spiders yet, which he had feared they would soon be housing. Just a dollop of bird mess on the roof.

'When are we gunna start the top layer?'

'Soon. But I was thinking . . . the poo looks like it's disappearing.'

Tomas peeked over at the pit. With the occasional rain shower and the fact the flies liked to eat the stuff, James was right.

'Top up?' Tomas suggested.

'We can do a quick sweep of the territory too,' James added.

With a plastic bag and a few choice sticks, they wandered along the Taff Trail. Tomas spoke about the film in all its glory – about the way the 3-D glasses made the X-Men seem real, like they were fighting right there in front of him. Solid. Touchable.

They wandered so far that they found themselves outside the graveyard on the mountainside. It looked dismal and dark in the dim light of the incoming storm.

'It gives me the creeps,' James shared with his friend, as he caught Tomas staring at the stones at the front of the yard.

'It *is* scary,' Tomas admitted. But he felt compelled to go in, like these were people who needed friends and gossip just as much as everyone else. He carried on walking towards the tall iron gates.

'Wait, we can't go in!'

'Why not?'

'I don't know anyone dead.'

'It doesn't matter,' Tomas said. 'We can still look.' His heart sped up and his body tingled with electricity. He was there now, so he might as well go inside. They'd spent enough time wandering around graveyards in zombie games – what difference did it make if he visited one for real?

'Fine. But if a hand comes out and grabs me, I'll poke them in the eye with my pooey-stick.'

Tomas nodded in understanding as his friend swung his smelly wooden weapon.

The graveyard was quiet, except for a lady in the distance. She had her hand pressed to a stone as the other wiped the black marble surface with a cloth. Tomas studied her, captivated by the love and care she was addressing the gravestone with. He couldn't understand why there weren't more people around doing the same thing. Some of the stones looked like they needed attention. They were wonky in the dirt and the words were mottled with age.

Finally, as Tomas scanned the area, he saw what he had been looking for. He recognised it from one of the pictures Eleri had put on the computer screen that night he'd slept over

– tall, white, arcing stones. He climbed the steep hill leading to them, with James loping behind.

'I'll keep my eyes peeled for zombies,' James announced, holding his stick like a shotgun. The Tesco Bag for Life, full of dog poo, swung from the crook of his arm.

Tomas reached out a hand and touched the white stone wall. The graves stretched in a big row, all identical in height. Someone had laid a fresh batch of wild daisies on the ground, and further along he spotted a bunch of coloured flowers he didn't know the names of.

'Who are they? Soldiers?' James asked, lowering his imaginary gun.

'No. It's those people Eleri was talking about. From the Aberfan Disaster.'

James squinted at the stones. 'They're so young. Some of them are younger than us.'

Tomas felt his chest swelling with sadness. Right here, on this hill, were children that had never had a chance to grow up. Never had a chance to finish school or to learn how to drive a car. Never got to have babies of their own and get jobs as firemen, nurses or astronauts.

Suddenly, the sky grumbled fiercely. Fat spots of rain landed on top of the boys' heads. Sharing a look of surprise and intrigue, they started back towards the gate at a run. But Tomas was caught off guard when he saw a new figure amongst the gravestones up ahead.

'It's him again,' he said in realisation, trying to catch his breath.

'What was that? I can't hear you,' James replied. Black clouds were pounding angrily into one another and thunder roared in the heavens.

'He's following me,' Tomas decided, glowering back at the stock-still boy, blatantly staring at them.

'Who's following you?' James turned his

head this way and that. 'A spy? Do you think they want our treehouse?'

Tomas felt as if something had clicked into place. Yes. That's precisely what he was starting to think. Either that, or the boy was lonely.

'Come on. If we run fast enough, we might lose him.' He took off, sprinting through the lashing rain as it bucketed down around them. His hair became slathered in it and his T-shirt got so wet, he could see the dip of his belly-button through the material.

They made a quick stop at the poo-pit to empty their fresh finds and then veered away, like boys possessed by wild spirits, cheering at the skies.

'I dunno when I'll be allowed out again next,' Tomas yelled through the hammering raindrops, when he was nearing his front door.

'That's okay. I'll knock for you when Mam

sets me free. It's going to be homework for the next few days I bet!'

Tomas thumped on the front door and stood waiting. He looked like a hippo in a river, his skin glistening. In the distance, James dashed madly across the road and slipped into the alley that led to his back garden.

Lightning lit up the world as the front door opened. Tomas' mam appeared with a bath towel in hand. 'I warned you didn't I, boyo?' she said, but she didn't sound angry. There was a glint in her eyes and as she wrapped him up into her arms, her dimples were showing.

Chapter Eight

IT RAINED for two days straight. Tomas had been holed up in his bedroom, writing about the battle of Hastings for his history lesson, writing a book review for English on *The Twits*, and drawing a picture for art of the things he had done on his holiday so far. In his sketch book he drew a tree with a little wooden house perched there, then a green coat, on which he creatively drew mice poking their little heads from the pockets. In the middle of the page he drew a nest of cushions and blankets with a torch and game controller on top. He left the other spaces on the page blank, just in case something amazing happened that he needed to add later.

On the second evening of his imprisonment due to bad weather, Tomas found his mam sat in the living room. She was watching the *Antiques Road Show* with a cup of coffee and a packet of chocolate digestives, which she instantly offered him. Tomas took a biscuit and was careful to hold his hand beneath the tasty morsel, catching the crumbs as they fell.

'I'm glad you're here. I need to talk to you.' She reached for the remote control and turned the television on mute.

The silence engulfed him. He didn't like tension. It made him fidget. He licked the crumbs off his palms and wiped his hands on his pyjamas. Then he reached for another biscuit, which he ate in little tiny bites.

'How would you feel if I started seeing someone?'

Tomas scrunched his nose up as if there

was a bad smell in the air, when in actual fact he could still detect the aroma of the lightly buttered toast his mam had had for supper.

'You mean a boyfriend?'

She gave a little nod. 'Yes, a . . . well . . . a boyfriend, if that's what you'd like to call it.'

Tomas had stopped nibbling the biscuit without realising it. 'What if Dad comes back?'

His mam chewed her lip and laced her fingers together nervously. 'Tommy . . . You know that, as much as I loved your father, if he came back we wouldn't be together anymore. It just wouldn't work for us now. Do you understand?'

Tomas averted his eyes. He couldn't look at her when he felt deeply miserable. 'I know. I just hoped.'

She reached over and squeezed his knee. 'I know, baby.'

Silence again.

'So, you found someone you like instead?' Tomas asked.

She smiled weakly. 'I think so. Yes.'

He nodded. 'Do I have to call him Dad?'

'Oh gosh, no! Don't be silly.' She gave a little high pitched laugh. 'You can call him by his first name.'

'Alright. Whatever.' He shrugged. 'It's your life, Mam.'

Surprise sparked in her eyes. 'Don't be angry, Tommy.'

'I'm not angry. And I'm not *Tommy*.' He put the half eaten biscuit on the edge of the sofa before getting up. Forgotten crumbs tumbled from his lap onto the burgundy carpet, but he didn't care. He was empty inside and didn't know how to fill the space.

Silence followed him to his bedroom.

Picking up the sketch book at his desk, he grabbed his pencil and furiously scribbled over the image of his new green coat. But the pencil lead snapped under the pressure and tore a hole in the paper, marking the blank sheet underneath.

He sighed loudly, then looked at the mess he'd made. His eyes wandered to the sketch of his treehouse in the corner of the page. Sitting inside the treehouse, in a sketchy, rough, mass of lines, was a boy, hunched, with his arms clutching his knees to his chest.

Tomas stared at the sketch in awe.

He hadn't drawn a *boy*.

So who had?

✶

On the third day it drizzled, but the sun tried to peek through the black clouds every now and again. Tomas had grown so bored, he begged his mam to let him visit James at his house. Reluctantly, she agreed as she stood over the ironing board in the kitchen, still in her white, fluffy dressing gown and slippers.

He'd asked during breakfast if she'd been in his room the night before and drawn on his picture. Her reaction was as he'd predicted: raised eyebrows and confusion.

'Nope. I can't draw,' she'd laughed, as she spooned out the pinky flesh of a grapefruit. 'You must have done it when you were half asleep.'

'Hmm,' he'd mumbled – because he didn't know what else to say on the matter.

James wasn't in the best of moods when Tomas arrived in his new coat with all the large pockets. It wasn't just because of the rain, either.

'Dad noticed the tools were missing. He's gone bananas,' he explained grimly.

Tomas felt like he'd swallowed a stone, which had lodged in his throat. He hated bad news, especially when he was a part of it somehow. James' dad worked for a bank and got easily irritated when things weren't in the places he'd left them. James had thrown one of his dad's motorcar magazines out with the old newspapers once, in a mad rush to assist the recycling men. It hadn't been a good day for him.

'He's grounded me.'

'Did you get the tools back for him?'

'No. He's stormed out. Said he was going to B&Q to buy new ones with my pocket money.'

Tomas made a hissing noise with his mouth. 'Sounds horrible.' He looked up and down the street in case he saw James' dad approaching in the car. 'Should I go home?'

'No. It's fine. He'll probably be nicer to me if you're here. But we'll have to stay in my room.' He opened the door wider and coaxed Tomas inside. They went straight upstairs, taking them two at a time.

James' bedroom was much tidier than it usually was. His X-Men figures were all balanced neatly on the shelf above his bed and his desk and cabinets had been dusted. All his shoes were neatly paired and poking out from under the bed. There was even a book spread open and upside down on the bedside table.

'What are you reading?'

'Some cack about a young spy. It's so unreal I stopped reading it. He doesn't even have any superpowers and yet he gets out of everything.'

'Maybe we could do with a few tips?' Tomas pointed out with a grin.

'I'd rather take on an army of giant aliens than my dad *any* day. Believe me.'

The games console was downstairs, so that was out of the question. James dug out a crushed Connect Four box from his cupboard instead and they played idly, not really caring who won. It was just something to keep their hands busy while they thought about all the things they'd *rather* be doing.

When a tap came at the door, they both looked at each other startled. It opened before James could say anything and his dad's body filled the gap in the doorway; blocking out all the light from the landing.

'Oh . . . Tomas . . . I had no idea you were here.'

'Sorry,' Tomas spluttered, straightening his back and sitting neatly with his legs crossed, as a sign of respect.

James' dad wafted a hand in his direction. 'No, it's okay, but James and his mam are going to do some food shopping now.'

James looked annoyed by the news. Apparently, he hadn't been aware of this.

'She can drop you home on the way if you'd like?'

Tomas was already clambering to his feet. 'It's okay. I feel like being outside. I'll speak to you soon, okay?' he said, turning to his friend, who was begrudgingly reaching for a pair of trainers under the bed.

'No worries,' he sulked. James hated shopping. He'd told Tomas on many occasions. He hated that his mam would hold up fruit or vegetables and ask if they looked okay to him – as if he *cared*!

The drizzle made Tomas' clothes clammy and heavy as he wove back down the alley, kicking stones. He'd only been gone over an hour and still the day stretched ahead. He knew the park would be empty – and no doubt everywhere else too – so he had little choice but to stick with his mam, as she spent her time cleaning surfaces and watching programmes like *Cash in the Attic*. Boring.

But Tomas was struck dumb when he saw something unusual outside his home.

At the side gate, leading to the garden, there sat a dog. A familiar, black-furred, long-tongued dog.

He shot a glance at the front door and hesitated. His mam rarely had visitors because she didn't really know anyone in the area. Samantha came once in a while when it was dry, because she was able to enjoy pushing her daughter Lois around in the pram, but it was unlikely she'd risk a stroll in the rain and wind.

Tomas, at last sucking in a deep breath, knocked on the front door. He could see the shape of his mam in the patterned glass and waited. She seemed to be taking longer than usual. He knocked again. She finally whipped the door open.

'Hey, baby,' she said. Her voice sounded off to him. Strained.

'That dog . . .' he began, but was interrupted by the appearance of a tall, skinny figure emerging from the living room.

'Hi there, Tomas. Rubbish weather, eh, boyo?'

Tomas looked at his mam, puzzled and suddenly suspicious.

'Daniel came over for a cup of tea. I've been losing my mind with boredom so he thought he'd save me,' she said hurriedly.

Tomas felt he was in a Mexican stand off. As if, any minute, he or Daniel would draw a pistol and aim for one another. He didn't like it. He felt like an animal, cornered in a pen.

'Why don't you come on through to the kitchen and Mammy will make you a sandwich. Then we can all talk.'

'Stop talking to me like I'm a baby!' Tomas snapped. He didn't know where his anger had come from, but it was there, building in his chest.

'I'm sorry, Tom. You're right. I shouldn't. But I like thinking of you as my little man.' She stroked his damp hair and then gestured for the boys to follow her.

'I can go if you like?' Daniel suggested to her in a hushed tone.

'No, it's okay. Perhaps now is as good a time as any to talk.'

Tomas thought she looked small and wilted as she stood in the doorway at the end of the hall. He followed her because he loved her, not because he wanted to know what she had to say.

At the table, Tomas eyed Daniel. The man was grinning from ear to ear and tapping his fingers on the table top. Silence hung between them as Tomas' mam pottered around the kitchen and when she returned with a ham and cheese sandwich – minus the usual lettuce and tomato – he noticed something different. She was wearing perfume. She smelt flowery and fresh. She had even changed out of her dressing gown into a peach blouse and denim jeans.

'Tomas . . . you remember our little chat the other night?' she started, as she slipped onto a chair.

He shrugged in a noncommittal way. They talked most nights. How was he to know which conversation she meant?

'About how you would feel if I had a boyfriend?'

His eyes became as big as Ferris wheels. '*This* is your boyfriend?'

She let out a nervous laugh and Daniel grinned like a cat about to leap on a little, defenceless mouse.

'See, Daniel and I really like each other . . . and . . . well . . . I'd like him to start spending time here with us.'

'No!' Tomas shouted, slapping a hand on the table.

His mam looked mortified by his outburst and Daniel's leg started bouncing up and down. Up and down. Up and down – his heels pat-pat-patting against the tiled floor.

'He's not staying here. Mam, he *can't.*' Tomas' mind whirled. His head raged. His heart was beating like the hooves of a galloping horse against dirt. No no no, it sang. Even his ears were burning as he stood up.

'I don't want you near my mam!' he yelled at Daniel.

'Tomas!' she exclaimed.

'Come on, boyo. I only want to treat your mam right and be a friend to you both –'

'Shut up!' he spat. 'Leave us alone!'

Daniel caught his mam's eye and he reached over to place a hand over the top of hers.

That was the moment.

That was the moment Tomas felt his chest explode and his legs start to pump towards the door.

He couldn't stay any longer.

He just couldn't.

Chapter Nine

THE SKY had opened up again. Rain battered the concrete and created little streams in the gutters. The grass was sodden and squelchy and the trees beckoned furiously to crows caught flying against the wind.

There were no dog walkers or bike riders on the Taff Trail, which Tomas was thankful for. Even with the rainwater on his face to wash away his tears, he couldn't help the little sounds of upset that escaped his mouth as he ran. It was embarrassing but he couldn't stop.

When his secret tree came into view, he

felt his anger shift and his relief blossom. He just wanted to sit and be quiet; alone. No Mam. No James. And especially no Daniel.

But what he saw, as he got even closer, took his breath away –

What he came upon made his chest tight and his skin crawl with a choking, overwhelming misery.

'No,' he whispered to himself.

How could they do this? How?

He leapt over the man-made poo pit that had clearly failed to ensnare intruders and landed amongst the demolished shards and planks of his creation. Someone had ripped the ladder clean off the tree and stomped on every little step, snapping it in pieces. The ground was littered with planks that had splintered and cracked with ease and a lot of the wood had been thrown down the hill into the ferns.

Tomas wiped his eyes quickly and kicked the ferns aside, looking for one of the hammers he'd hidden. The tools were still there, covered in mud. As he reached for it, he noticed a discarded cigarette butt lying on the earth. He squashed the butt into the mud with his foot and reached for a plank of wood that looked reasonably intact. Then, grabbing onto a tree branch, he propelled himself upwards and onto the remains of the base of his treehouse.

The planks that had been left in place groaned under his trainers. In desperation, Tomas frantically hammered wood back into place.

Faster, faster, his hammer struck the nails that were still poking through.

When the piece was in, he stood up, ready to salvage another discarded plank. But the plank he was already standing on made an almighty snapping sound. His arms flailed out and his body went over the edge, breaking twigs and flapping through the air uselessly.

And as he struck the pile of debris below, he felt a sharp, burning sensation pierce into his back.

*

The dream stuff of heaven always tugged at Anthony when he left it. As magnificent and peaceful as it was there, the mischievous child in him was too curious to stay in one place forever. Sometimes he liked to go back just to watch and see the world changing. It was a free land to him, a place where he could witness anything if he happened to be in the right place.

If he concentrated really hard, he could touch things and influence them, somehow. He'd visited Tomas in his sleep to share his story. He had also sensed from the lingering, swooping trails of angel dust that something was going to happen here, in Aberfan. Something that could change Tomas' life.

That's why he stayed, just for a little while.

When he saw Tomas flee his mam's home in tears, he followed. He watched Tomas discover the horrible mess his wonderful treehouse had been left in by teenage vandals. He saw the anger inside Tomas as he climbed the tree and started to build it again out of despair.

And when Tomas slipped over the edge with the alarming echo of a SNAP, Anthony dived towards the wood Tomas was about to land on and pushed it with all his might . . . just an inch. But it was enough.

It was enough.

＊

Tomas lay looking at the sky through the branches of his not-so-secret tree. The rain splattered against his nose and eyelids – even plopped into his mouth as he blinked it from his eyes.

He couldn't move. The pain was too much. His vision blurred in and out as waves of agony juddered through his body.

As time drifted, he heard a scuffling sound.

He looked and saw a face – at least he thought he did. He couldn't focus properly, and with the light above so bright, he wasn't sure if his mind was playing tricks.

Then, something solid brushed against his face. He could hear his name being called in the distance.

Carefully he lifted a hand to the sleek wet fur of a jet-black dog that was snuffling his face contentedly.

'I'm here!' Tomas croaked.

'I've got him, Carys,' came a cry, as Daniel tore through the bushes. He pushed his dog aside gently and knelt down amongst the debris.

'Ow! OW, don't move me!' Tomas begged. 'Please don't touch me. My back –'

'Oh, baby!' his mam sobbed as she came into view.

Daniel already had his mobile in hand and with a calm voice asked for an ambulance.

'You're going to be okay,' his mam promised, stroking his cheek with tears in her eyes. 'We're here now.'

She kissed the top of his head repeatedly, trying to shield his face from the rain with her body. Tomas held her hand and squeezed it. A part of him was afraid. But another part of him listened to his mam's voice and believed her words with a shudder of relief. As long as he had her close, he would be fine.

Chapter Ten

TOMAS PEELED open one eye. The light outside the window was bright and crisp. He noticed there were blinds instead of net curtains, which struck him as odd. This wasn't his home. This wasn't his bedroom.

'Mam?' he whispered – for whispering was all he could manage.

'Tommy,' she replied.

He turned his aching head to the side and found her there, in a tall-backed chair with a heavily thumbed magazine on her lap. She dropped the magazine on the bedside table and sat on the edge of the bed, placing a hand comfortingly over his belly.

'I'm sorry . . . about . . .'

'It's okay,' she shushed him. Tears had sprung to her eyes. She looked tired. More tired than usual. The bags under her eyes were vivid and her hair looked messy. She wasn't even wearing make-up and there was no hint of the flowery perfume on her skin anymore.

'You've been sleeping a lot,' she explained. 'All that rain and damp sunk right into your skin. No wonder you went out like a light when the nurses put a blanket over you.' She tried for a warm smile but it dissolved into clear concern.

'What happened? When I fell? I couldn't move properly.'

She nodded. 'You landed on a nail. Still attached to some wood. They said it just missed your spine.' A tear slipped out at last – one single bead of salt water, trailing down her pale cheek. 'They said you were lucky. Any closer . . .' She choked on her words, and as Tomas processed this, a distraction came in the form of two familiar faces.

'All right, Tom?' James said, glancing gingerly between him and Tomas' mam as he bustled into the room with his own Mam in tow. He stood awkwardly in the corner; hands stuffed in his camouflage-coloured trouser pockets.

'The treehouse is gone,' Tomas mumbled. He had dreaded this moment: the moment he would have to tell his friend that their world of childish secrets and play had been stolen from them. He tried to sit up but a searing pain in his back made him pause. He decided he was better off where he was, even if it did feel a little rude to be lying flat.

'That's okay. I don't think we'll be allowed around a hammer and nails for a while,' James said with a jovial air, though he did look at his mam, expecting a scolding remark. It didn't come, however.

'Nothing lasts, does it?' Tomas sighed.

'There are too many people who enjoy being destructive,' James' mam piped up from the doorway. 'They have nothing better to do around here.'

'I just hope you get better soon. I'm going to be *so* frickin' bored without you around. Elori asked me to paint her nails last night and I actually said yes.'

The women laughed. Tomas smiled, imagining his friend hunching over his sister's hand with a sparkly nail polish and trying his hardest to get it perfect, or else she'd clip him across the head.

'We brought you this. It's a Simpsons comic. It's quite funny. I read some in the car on the way over.' James accepted a magazine from his mam and passed it over to his friend.

'Thanks,' Tomas smiled appreciatively.

He was later told he had to stay in the hospital to be monitored, even though he could move his legs without any problems. Other than a stiff, painful back he was fine. He wondered if this was how his grandparents had felt every day, moving around with a slight hunch on unsteady feet. It wasn't nice, that was for sure.

When his mam came to visit, she was always quick to talk about the weather outside and the programmes she'd watched, if Tomas had nothing to say himself. It was hard to have any news when the ceiling was your main point of focus.

He noticed she was careful not to mention Daniel and it bugged him a little. He wanted her to bring him up so he didn't have to. But in the end, he took the plunge.

'Mam?'

'Yes?'

'I'm sorry I got so angry about Daniel.'

She waved a hand of dismissal. 'Don't

worry yourself over that. I just need you to get better.'

'I know,' he said, and then sucked in a deep breath. 'But I need you to be happy too, Mam.'

She looked frozen in her chair all of a sudden, and wooden like a puppet.

'Don't stop seeing him,' he added.

A little smile cracked in the corner of her mouth. 'That's really mature of you,' she said at last. 'You have no idea how much of a weight just came off my shoulders. You know, he's been dying to come and see that you're okay, but I told him to keep his distance while you were getting better.'

Tomas had thought this was the case. His mam had left occasionally to answer calls that sounded like updates on his health.

'He can come if he wants,' he said.

His mam touched his shoulder and a warm, dimpled smile spread fully across her lips at last. 'We've got all the time in the world for you to get to know each other.'

*

When Tomas was back home, he couldn't wait to lay in his own bed, with his own things all around him and to drink a proper cup of hot chocolate made by his mam. She had promised to bring him one in his favourite Spiderman mug just as soon as he'd taken his bits and bobs from the hospital up to his room.

His bed was made and his room looked spotless, which he hadn't expected. For all the time his mam had been at the hospital, he was surprised she'd had the time to clean anything!

Dropping his Simpsons comic – and all the other magazines he'd been given – onto his desk, he looked down at his sketchbook, still left open. The sheet of paper he'd scribbled over in anger was there. The same sheet on which the mysterious sketch of a boy had appeared.

Curiously, he picked it up and took a closer look. The boy was so small, he really couldn't make out any defining details, no matter how hard he squinted.

Sighing, he tore the sheet away. He would have to draw a new picture for his homework – maybe something scarily real, like a boy with a plank of wood accidentally nailed to his back.

As he placed the sketchbook back down on the desk, he almost didn't notice it at first. His brain told him the mark on the page was the result of his pencil piercing the sheet above. But as he turned away, the mark formed more clearly in his mind and he snapped his head back.

It wasn't his pencil coming through the top sheet at all.

It was words.

Tomas stared at it and felt his stomach somersault.

He read the message over and over.

He knew that name from his dreams.

Live

Love

Make every day count

Anthony x

First, his veins sizzled with a strange sort of terror. Then his heart, as it slowed back to its normal pulsing rhythm, whispered to him: *Don't be afraid. This is a miracle. An angel is watching over you. He's someone very young, and extraordinarily special.*

Listen to him . . .

Don't let him down . . .